MW00737384

OTHER BOOKS BY JAY LAKE

THE SPECIFIC
GRAVITY OF GRIEF

JAY LAKE

THE SPECIFIC
GRAVITY
OF GRIEF

JAY LAKE

FAIRWOOD PRESS
Bonney Lake, WA

THE SPECIFIC GRAVITY OF GRIEF

A Fairwood Press Book

Copyright © 2010 by Joseph E. Lake, Jr.

Fairwood Press
21528 104th Street Ct E
Bonney Lake WA 98391

See all our titles at:
www.fairwoodpress.com

Cover image by Kyle Cassidy
Book Design by Patrick Swenson

ISBN: 978-1-933846-57-6
First Fairwood Press edition: June 2010
First trade paperback edition: February 2016
Printed in the United States of America

Cancer has stolen so much from my life, and given so much back. I owe my life, love, and liberty to Shannon Page, Shelly Rae Clift, my Child, and my entire family. Thanks to all who have given me so much.

FOREWORD
J.A. Pitts

My friend Jay Lake published this book in June of 2010 as a great big fuck you to cancer. He had already had some surgeries and was in store for more, whether he knew it at the time or not. His last few years were a rollercoaster of love and loss, pain and hope, wishful thinking, and hard, cutting edge scientific exploration.

Yep, Jay was one of the first civilians to have his genome sequenced. With the help of some amazing friends, he ran a fundraising campaign to have both his DNA and RNA sequenced. This was such a unique request, the scientists who sequenced his DNA had no process for figuring out how to charge for the activity, but they worked it out.

In the end of this exploration, Jay was able to give the world a unique look into the formation and sequencing of his cancer tumors and allow for new avenues of thought on treatment. His final push was to get into a gene therapy—

specifically around his white blood cells—with the National Institute of Health. He knew it was a Hail Mary pass, but was willing to trust science to the very end. While the findings were hopeful, in the end it was not enough. We lost Jay on June 1st, 2014, just days before his fiftieth birthday. He left a huge hole in a lot of hearts.

Jay believed in science. Tooth and nail, heart and soul, he believed that with enough study, insight, and experimentation, we could unravel not only the cure for cancer, but the very heart of the universe. Ignorance was abhorrent to him.

When he titled this book *The Specific Gravity of Grief*, he did not choose those words just because they sounded cool. The title evokes the juxtaposition of the scientific against the emotive. Grief is not measurable; we cannot explain it in numbers or rational theory. Jay sought to explore that incongruity, to help find a language to understand something that eluded him.

Specific gravity is the ratio of the density of a substance to the density of a reference substance; equivalently, it is the ratio of the mass of a substance to the mass of a reference substance for the same given volume.

Basically, Jay understood the world to be a certain way, and he was struggling to understand the ratio of grief to that world view.

This book is a fantasy—one where a fictional Jay Lake survives cancer but manages to alienate those he loves. He and I discussed the content of this book many, many times. It reflects his anguish over his writing career, the struggle to be a good parent, and the constant work required to have grown up relationships when his world was falling down around him.

Do not believe for an instant that this is a book about joyous validation or miracles. It is full of hope and pain, self-loathing, and a grudging acceptance of one's place in the universe.

This is a roadmap of one man's attempt to survive the deterioration of his very existence and how he imagined one could live, despite the worst.

Jay was my friend. I hate that I can no longer call him, hear his laughter, groan at his inappropriate remarks, and love him for his foibles and his remarkable humanity. We have his memories, but frankly, those are just not enough.

Not like we got a vote.

I was Jay's truth-teller, his secret keeper. He would talk to me about the darkness and the fear because he understood I would help him see the light. Our phone calls more often than not began with pain, but by the end would culminate with laughter or the relief of tears.

If you would know the road ahead, read this book. If you fear the dark, read this book. If you have a loved one who is struggling, read this book. Jay was a brilliant writer. You will not regret this journey.

—John A Pitts, 2016

INTRODUCTION
Maureen McHugh

In late winter of 2005, I walked into a hospital waiting room. I said hello to the receptionist and without bothering to go to the desk, said my last name and that I was the 11:00. Around a corner of a little alcove to a doorway was a magazine rack, one of two in the office. Because the door led back to the labs and all the testing gear for echo cardiograms, CT scans, all the elaborate ways to examine the lungs and hearts and lord knows what else, patients would often get to the door and realize that they were still carrying their magazine. So all the good magazines tended to end up there. But since the magazine rack wasn't particularly visible from the door, most patients tended not to notice it when they came in.

I'd been here several times for bunches of different tests. I was here now for a CT scan. I'd drink a contrast drink (a liter and then wait for, if I remember, half an hour) and then have my scan. Then I'd have a light lunch, and after that I'd have chemo in the afternoon. I had my bag of chemo distractions—books, a notebook a magazine. Most days when I was going out in public I wore a wig. I carefully drew in eyebrows, and used eyeliner so that behind my glasses you registered something like eyelashes. You would not have noticed anything about me unless you knew me, and then you probably would have wondered why I looked so much better, so much more put together, than I usually do. But on chemo days, I was going to sit in the infusion center for four hours and I was going to be comfortable. I just wore a scarf over my obviously bald head.

The receptionist didn't need me at the desk because she had to get the contrast started anyway, and I'd hand her my insurance card then. People griped about the contrast drink and it wasn't great. Sort of like a weird diet/lemonade/energy drink. But it was no big deal.

I scored some trash magazines and turned around and *every person sitting in the waiting room instantly averted their eyes*. Most of the people in the waiting room were getting a test so their doctor could make a diagnosis. I obviously already had my diagnosis. They had been staring at me, a native of this strange place, so familiar with the rituals of the hospital, so marked by chemotherapy. I was their nightmare. A walking *momento mori*. I had cancer.

I had Hodgkins Lymphoma. Stage III Nodular sclerosis, type A, which is to say that I had no night sweats or itching and my disease was not classified as "bulky." Cancer of the lymph nodes. (It is a highly treatable cancer, and has a 75% cure rate. In three months, I will have been cancer free for five years, and officially not in remission, but cured.) I had read Susan Sontag's *Illness as Metaphor* years before. I recognized that in literature, cancer is often a metaphor for a creeping inner spiritual rot, or any sort of curse. It is a punishment. It is an example of the capriciousness of fate. I had found that cancer in my life was much less metaphorical. What I had not been prepared for was to be turned into a walking metaphor myself. That with my eyebrowless, eyelashless face, in its boiled egg nakedness, I would become, like cancer, a metaphor for death.

What Jay Lake writes is a way to deal with life. With his own cancer diagnosis he has written something of a memoir. This isn't a memoir of Jay's actual life, although there are parallels with it. The protagonist is a writer who when he wrote had the same writing habits as Jay. But Jay's daughter is fine. Like many of the significant moments of life, say, the birth of a child or a parent's aging, life-threatening illness makes us consider what is going to happen. There's a cancer culture. It emphasizes support groups, optimism, and names sick people "cancer survivors." People pray or visualize chemo destroying their cancer cells. They practice good thinking. Maybe some of them remain completely and determinedly certain that they will be fine.

For the rest of us, there are considerations. What if the disease doesn't respond to treatment? What if it doesn't come back? How far will I go? How much pain will I endure? What will this do to the people I love? There aren't a lot of opportunities to air these scenarios. No one wants to talk about it. No one wants to think about it, certainly not the friends who are so determinedly being a support group. Certainly not the people in the waiting room where I was waiting before my CT scan, many of whom were thinking over and over, "don't let it be cancer."

Jay has made sympathetic magic. He has imagined a life devastated by cancer, in not one, but several ways. He has written into the darkness. People always say to young writers, "write what you know." But the truth is that we write about the big things in our lives that we don't know. We write to figure out what things mean. What shape they have. This is, like the P.E.T. scan described, a way of measuring cancer. It doesn't measure millimeters of tumor, but it does attempt to measure the emotional scope of disease. It is a kind of rehearsal for a play no one wants to star in. It is an exorcism. And like all magics and exorcisms, it is rooted deeply in metaphor.

There are places, journeys, that can't be directly described. This is a map of one of them.

THE SPECIFIC
GRAVITY
OF GRIEF

0.92; FAT

Death is as inevitable as springtime. Every windblown seed bears its own destruction written in telomeres and the ticking of a metabolic clock. Nothing in the world is forever—to be forever is to be timeless, and timelessness is stasis. Only in the tension between the first spark and the last crumbling ash could ambition ever be said to flourish.

He moves, our ragged man, like someone whose joints have been restrung by the crafts circle at a halfway house. Walks down the street avoiding the cracks in the sidewalk without conscious effort. The black burbling sealer between the squares has come unstrung through winter's harsh tutelage and lurks now for the unwary toe, the poorly balanced, the vestibularly challenged. Air is bracing, wind whistles the last song of ice and misery being banished by the northward-creeping sun, but still the danger is not quite over. Already flowers bloom like madness in a lover's eyes, but then, the colors almost always run from the green ground toward the blue sky in these Pacific Northwest climes.

So our man lurches a bit before straightening himself with a self-conscious glance to see who might be mocking. Only the uncaring birds observe, but their minds are so narrow and violent that they carry no space that he might inhabit any longer than receding threat would have it. A suspicious, resentful cat might have been more in keeping with the mood of the moment, but then, the mood was *his* and so was the moment.

This, then, is his progress. Never quite stumbling, never quite wrong, but never quite right. Someone watching with more intent than the fluttering sparrows and the scornful jays might wonder what they saw. The curious might make a list such as this:

- Multiple sclerosis
- Osteoarthritis
- Poorly healed trauma
- Joint replacement gone badly wrong

The curious might then put their pen away, heedless of a smear of ink across the web of one thumb, and wander off in search of a nonfat double latte. A moment of early spring crispness in the air, and the ragged man forgotten, just like any other random stranger of little note and less importance.

He himself is incurious. Not a maker of lists, not any more, though in his time he was a great one. Once. Now he progresses down the sidewalk, a shuddering limping pass through a neighborhood that might once have been his, that might once have hosted his dreaming.

★

This is the ragged man's dream, from a time before:

A house, wrapped in a sepia European light, as if a Flemish Old Master had spilled his paint box across the evening sky. The halls are unreasonably long and narrow, architectural arteriosclerosis, so that the visitor must shuffle almost sideways to pass from one throbbing chamber to the next. Electricity drips from the

sockets and fixtures to pool in sly, blue vague-
nesses at the corners of his vision.

Memory persists even so.

Once they ran laughing through these
halls, when the walls were wider and the floors
gleamed with bright promise. Once they sat
in companionable silence in the large kitchen
with the dangling pots as tomatoes gave their
all in steaming agony for a dinner (n)ever to
be forgotten. Once they climbed up to the
roof and lay their backs upon the day-warmed
composite shingles and watched shooting stars,
counting wishes like horses in a morning field.

He walks slowly onto a porch that has
somehow morphed to the dimensions of a
subway station, complete with screeching
rails and crackling announcements in some
incomprehensible tongue. Commuters in
their hundreds lounge on rocking chairs and
swings, each wearing clothing he might have
once owned.

Such a dangerous word, "once."

They smile, these men and women, their
faces moving in unison as if controlled by a
single set of invisible wires. Inside the house, a
kettle shrieks. Or perhaps a child. He turns to

go back, and finds the door sealed against him, nothing but siding where a moment before the entrance had stood. Peeling paint testifies to the age of this imprisonment of his memories. The windows, too, when he looks, are blank with wood.

Sealed, all sealed. He pounds the wall a while, amiable commuters nodding in rhythm to his fists, but no one comes. No one comes at all.

The ragged man finally reaches a bench in the shade of a maple tree. He sits down. The metal slats are cold through the rough wool of his pants. The back of the bench is not designed to accommodate the curvature of the human spine, any more than the world is designed to accommodate the curvature of the human heart.

He feels the small gaps in his support, cracks much larger than the sidewalk and as unavoidable as sin or sleep. Empty air gapes, a gulf between his thighs and the grass below, behind his ribs opening up onto the Little

League ball field where aluminum bats ring like a blow to the head and a frustrated coach has to remind children of boundless energy to run, run, run.

Once, the ragged man used to run. His blood still does. At that thought, he extends his left arm, rolls up the flopping sleeve of the rust-colored Old Navy sweater with his right hand, and studies the scars on his veins.

They are small, readily mistaken for freckles or the last gasp of some stray pimple decades after the lusty springtime of its fellows. They do not feel knotty or rough to the touch. At most, tiny lacunae in the sagging continuity of his skin, cousins to the little tags that erupt across the yoke of his shoulders, at which he picks in the shower when the self-conscious grooming becomes too much and he must not bloody his fingernails any further.

Flaws, tiny flaws visible to the discerning eye and the desperate mind.

Each scar marks an entry point, a violation, the bloody thrust of a needle laying bare his secrets and opening the plumbing of his heart to gloved hands and tingling drugs. He remembers CT scans, with their hot flush of the veins, the loosening of the bowels, the sexual thrill wrapped in the embarrassing, embracing cold of sterile rooms and beige plastic machines far bigger and more capable than he will ever be again. Scars on the skin, scars on the veins, so when he goes back, as he must like a child to terror, they hurt him ever more looking for some unused portal.

He tries to make a map of the scars, his idle mind seeking patterns as anyone might do in the rifting of clouds or the arrangement of stars in the night sky. *Pareidola?* No, that is the seeking of faces. Just pattern recognition, the same mild obsession that must solve the sequence of tiles in a strange bathroom or work out the handedness of the mason who built a fireplace. The human mind, unwilling to let chaos be chaos, must bring form from the void. How else to explain dreams?

Still, they are a map. Not of space, but time, a chart of the paths of pain through the hours and days of suffering. Even now, the ragged man can point to the scars one by one and name the procedure, the incident, the emergency that engendered the medical intervention in question. Sometimes he can remember the nurse, the IV therapist, the phlebotomist. Their faces are another kind of map, stretching from the countries of kindness to the swamps of indifference. (It seemed the women always liked him more when he was not crying.)

The ragged man studies this map, draws in memory like a net full of fish. Each individual thought slips away to flop silver-scaled on the decks of imagination, but still the mass is present, ever present, a weight across his back.

The first time he had tissue taken away and understood what it was he gave up was in a doctor's office in southeast Portland. A mole upon his neck, longtime irritation to shirt collars and sweaty days. Another in the middle of his back, that attracted needle-teethed fish to nip when he swam in rivers and oceans. The doctor used an electric wand—no needles in his life back then—and he'd thoughtlessly set his heels against the pedestal of the exam table, so that the circuit closed when she touched him, and he kicked the medical assistant.

After brief confusion and a short colloquy on electrical grounding, she'd resumed her work. Sparky, sharp moments later, two tiny pieces of him lay on cotton in a tray. Black heads, pink and tender roots, and the faint scent of burning meat. He looked, his hand raised to touch his neck, until shooed away by the doctor, then he mourned. For years after, he regretted not asking for the moles in a little jar. Flesh of his flesh, discarded for vanity and convenience. He felt foolish to mourn them. That was only the beginning, of loss and of grief, but it was enough for the time.

The cold park bench brings the ragged man back to the present. The pattern of his IV scars becomes once more a drunkard's walk of skin spots, as if it were his liver failing instead of his whole body. He stares up at the wispy cirrus clouds, like spider webs entrapping souls lately fled toward heaven, and tries to tell God he is still not ready.

God, as is His wont, gives no sign of having heard.

★

Fat floats, and when we have enough of it, carries us with it. Fat stores vitamins and poisons and everything needful and needless between, much like memory itself. Fat makes the delightful curves of a woman, and the sad middle-aged gut of a man. Fat is carved away by the knife of disease, until what remains is a stark, uncompromising warning for all good citizens to turn away.

0.94; LUNGS

He was born, as almost everyone is, quite young and quite surprised. Her first view of the world was blinding light and bracing cold. Strangely enough that would also be her last, but this is not that tale. Not now, not yet.

To be birthed is to breathe. To draw breath is to draw in life, gathering the world into you the first time, emerging as our distantmost ancestors once did from the salty pools of evolution. Ontogeny recapitulates phylogeny, from the blastocyte to the newborn, but even thereafter in the development of human behaviors in the juvenile East African plains ape. She acquired basic motor skills, depth perception, object permanence and the first glimmerings of abstract thought all too quickly.

The basic tools of childrearing are listening and love. The basic tools of the growing child are kinetic energy and an unerring talent for dangerous mistakes. Of this intersection is parenting born. She was listened to and loved, as only a daughter of the heart can be. She cannoned through her early years like a loose ball of twelve-pound shot, finding her way into ever deeper holes and toward ever brighter fires.

She grew, gathering life to her with a manic dedication that did not go unremarked by the world around her. "Old soul," they called her. "Wise." Sometimes, "dangerous," but that accusation always rendered with a tolerant smile. "Too much," "a handful," "how do you do it?"

Always she breathed. Always she took in the air around her, air that had passed through the lips of her parents, her friends, Jesus, Elvis, the Mahatma and lost Enkidu himself.

The human lung draws approximately 1.23 x 10(23) molecules of air with each breath. Almost 10(11) human beings have ever walked the earth. That leaves almost a trillion molecules per person in human history. Everyone who ever lived has breathed some of the air passing through your lungs right now.

Always the air made her more than she was, added to her height, her bulk, her mass, her wit, her strength, so that surely as any redwood grown from a seed she became tall and strong and generous and glorious. Words made flesh, the quadribecedarian code of the elastic, plastic genes building themselves out from germline to cellular scaffolding to willowy young woman so lithe and unsure, so innocent and sensual, so *alive*.

All from that first leap into the light, that first whimpering breath, that first cold, frightened moment.

All a lie.

★

Some fates lie in the hands of the gods. Or lightning. Or the weak patch in a truck tire. Some fates lie in the hands of sinners. Or saints. Or line judges who don't turn fast enough as a knife-wielding yob jumps a chain-link fence and runs across a field. Some fates are justice incarnate. Some are blind. Some are meted out by the mustard seed. Some are dumped by the cubic yard.

Few fates are foreseen, and fewer still are deserved. But those fates which emerge from the same germline that build the house of flesh are the most bitter of all, for they are the betrayal of parentage, the default of inheritance, the death of hope and the abrogation of futurity. When the story writ within the skin and bones is corrupted, *sui generis*, everything known and hoped and believed about the body and life is played false.

An error develops in the tiny words that build the proteins that make up a body. A mistake, a typo, transcription failure, a copy edit blooper replicated a few thousand times until something new grows. No different from a blastocyte, really, a zygote of corruption, that robs the heart and soul right out of the host.

No one can say why, not ever. The genes themselves? Environment? Heredity? Lifestyle? Poison? Cosmic rays? Luck? If only our chromosomes were large enough to require shotguns to mutate. The genes would not be so plastic then, the processes not so elastic. But no, we are trapped with the angel-trod pinheads that write out the codes of our life. One divine misstep turns a letter over and a tumor is born.

Just as a child does, the tumor grows inside

the body. Cells beget cells, arrange themselves thus and so to please the selfish demands of the rearranged genes. Structure emerges, resources are consumed, and slowly the host's entire existence becomes bound up in the parasite within.

So it was with her, this child, your child. Perhaps you should have checked the drinking water. Perhaps you should have thought about the fact that four members of the family next door had died of the cancer within five years of your child's birth. Perhaps you should have looked up from your nearly perfect, nearly successful, nearly urban life and wondered about what might happen.

But medical science won't provide CT scans on children—unnecessary testing carries too much risk, even if the risk is a chance to survive. It wouldn't have helped if you had asked, not until everything had gone on far too long, far too late, far too much.

When your sweet, smart, strong child with her little parasite finally went before the beige battalions of testing equipment, it was already past time. For you. For her mother. For anyone. Damage done perhaps even before she was born resided in her like a snake wrapped around the last egg in the nest.

Ask yourself, how did you feel when they first told you? It's a simple question, really.

```
a)   Numb
b)   Disbelieving
c)   Ashamed
d)   Afraid
e)   Sick
f)   Angry
g)   You never felt again
```

There is a special distance, between the eyes of a parent and the eyes of a child. Small enough for the Casimir effect to take place, large enough that the very gulfs of time are uncrossable. You always see your child with Schroedingerian eyes, present and not-present, her currency and her futurity combined in one web of potential. In the face of diagnosis, those probabilities collapse, and you wonder how large a hole must be dug to lay her body down.

You know you should cry, but the tears have been starved from you. You know you should rage, but a broken hearth holds no fires. You know so many things, and none of them are true. None of them at all except this:

Your child has cancer. And she will not get better.

In time, when you leave, you drive home. Hands mindless on the wheel. Eyes blindly not-looking at the road. Mouth gaping as if some word could come out that might help, that might calm your wife's quiet weeping, as if a mere combination of syllables could be large enough, powerful enough, divine enough, to rip the vile truth from your minds, from her flesh and bones, from the world itself.

If you could eat suns, you would first swallow cancer, and let its terror die in the hydrogen fires that light the world.

If you could boil oceans, you would sink cancer into that saltwater embrace before sublimating all your grief to steam.

If you could crush evil with a mere step of your foot, you would spread cancer as wide and naked as a roasting chicken in the pan, then smash it to worthless paste.

Instead you drive through a day that is obnoxiously, uncaringly, indifferently beautiful,

as if the birds in the trees do not know what
has been lost.

Some fates lie in the hands of the god, but
some fates you have birthed yourself, built gene
by gene from the flesh of your own flesh. Some
fates are too simple and easy to be denied.

The lungs hold life-giving air, and give out
gasses that would choke you in a dozen breaths.
They power speech, and are the foundation
for sobs of grief. Even they grow illegitimate
children to be excised by the subtle hands of
surgeons, and in doing so betray every breath
in your body.

1.007; CEREBROSPINAL FLUID

The ragged man sits and rings the changes of his life. Deaths, dyings, tests, retests, pains and suffering beyond a reasonable man's allotment. Or even an unreasonable man's allotment.

He is walking again now, always moving just a little ahead of the pale horse that has been lurking at the corner of his vision these past few years. Death is patient as the dawn—its turn will always come, no matter how fast one runs. Still, running is better than gasping by the side of the road in depressed abandon.

So he walks, and thinks about all the times life changed and changed again.

Once, when it had still been possible to find humor, he used to refer to the Nuclear Medicine unit as the Department of Giant Radioactive Spiders. From the outside, Nuclear Medicine was a hushed waiting room full of the ill and their desperate loved ones. The ladies at the desk knew too many of their names, watched them walk in week after week more wilted each time, like a giant, fleshly produce display going to rot in slow motion. He had not become one of those names—radiation therapy had never been indicated for his complex of cancers. Only that he must have a PET scan periodically, looking for the secrets of dark growing things deep within the ragged man's body.

Positron Emission Tomography. Big gray and beige donuts in low-lit rooms with whirring fans and the hushed voices of nurses and techs. But that isn't the interesting part. More tedious than a CT scan, less frightening than an MRI, the interesting part about the PET scan is the prep.

The ragged man always said, watch out for any medicine that comes in a lead case. The prep nurse would sidle into the room lugging something about the size of a shoebox that obviously weighed several dozen pounds. Handling it with more care than a bag of anthrax, she would pull out a tungsten-jacketed syringe straight out of some 1970s exploitation torture film. Lurking within was a fluid the color of

Gatorade, the carrier for radioactively-tagged glucose analogs.

Giant radioactive spiders in a narrow tube, needle-fed into the ragged man's veins so he could sit quietly in a dark room for an hour while the metabolically active parts of his body could take up their allotments—brain, heart, bladder, tumor.

Cancer was a lifestyle with as many nuances as any other. He'd first learned it through his daughter, before later becoming a convert in his own right. For a long time, he rarely spoke of it, at least not outside small, windowless exam rooms dominated by sphygmomanometers on the wall and posters about tuberculosis or natural childbirth or the value of vaccination. Some secrets were meant to be kept. Some conversations killed themselves before they ever began.

Back then, when the ragged man still had a wife, when his daughter still had a mother, even their conversations were limited to quiet whispers and elliptical allusions. They did not want to frighten the girl, they did not want to say the word "neuroblastoma" lest the power of the thing be made even more manifest in her body, in the world, in the rotting chambers of their hearts. Too much to take in, too much to contain, too much to allow the reality of.

Later, when so much had been lost, then he'd been told how much more there was to lose—beyond even the ragged man's worst, wildest expectations—he found the shape of his words. "Tubulovillous adenocarcinoma" was an early favorite.

Once more in memory, an earlier time, when the tally of the scars had only just begun, a pack of doctors shuffled into his hospital room. Sunlight flooded the windows, so the place was strangely bright, even compelling in its beauty—whites and grays folded in on one another, an origami of gauze and sheets and curtains and IV tubing strangely pleasing to the eye.

It was a teaching hospital—Oregon's medical school, really—and so the pack was doctors ranging from a barely formed medical student not yet annealed in the first firing of his degreed education all the way to a grizzled attending physician with a fatherly manner and a distracted air, whose hands spoke of the competence of any long-practiced craftsman.

They huddled, staring, wide-eyed as a tree full of owls.

He waited, knowing that good news came quickly with a smile, but bad news traveled on many reluctant feet.

"Cancer," they muttered, their voices oddly passive and avoiding any assignment of blame or responsibility or even, truly, agency. "We're so very sorry. Completely treatable. Young. Healthy." This mantra passed from mouth to mouth as if the five physicians shared a single thought that could not be forced out in one go.

I have been here before, the ragged man thought as the doors of his grief opened up and swallowed him down into the darkness beneath, whole and screaming and grave-silent.

Their lips continued to move, the sunlight continued to flood the room with the false cheer of springtime, words rained down upon him Noachian in their density and depth, but he was gone now, down a road that began with a summer fever and ended by the side of a muddy grave.

If it had ever ended, because now he stood once more with his feet upon the road, its mud curdling to bloody, raw lips around his feet, looking down into the dankness of grief, ruin and despair.

Eventually, the doctors stopped talking and went away. They left him with a small drawing of the inside of his colon. The cartoon tumor looked almost cheerful, like a life-giving videogame mushroom. He imagined it with lambent eyes and a shy, girlish smile. He wanted to sing, "The shit flows, the shit flows out, the tumor stirs it all about . . ."

Had he agreed to something? He didn't know. The needles in his arms were only the beginning. He knew what their bright-fanged, narrow-bodied bastardy had done to his child.

Welcome to the lifestyle of cancer. Here's your ration of grief. Please try to throw up in the wastebasket. Terror seminars at 11 am and 3 pm. Mourners form a double line to the left to kiss you on your paper cheek before you slide away on an ocean of spaded dirt and fumbled cigarette butts.

★

The ragged man sets that memory aside and considers what else he has lost. The tragedies of his life always seem to come in springtime, as if their seeds had lain beneath winter frost until warmth and moisture had brought forth germination. Today's sunlight bears that same mocking brilliance of memory of his first diagnosis.

Thank god they had buried his daughter in the late winter rains. To encumber the memory of *that* loss with every bird-lilting sunny day would have scarred his heart beyond redemption. Not that he does so well in any case.

He studies the papery skin of his hands, how the knuckles almost glow beneath, where the pain shows through like a score being kept in gleaming ivory tokens. The nails are strange and brittle, though that is more likely poor nutrition and failing health than the fault of any of the wonder drugs in his oncologist's toxophilic quiver. These hands once belonged to a lover of women, a cooker of food, a writer of stories. These hands once wrenched spark-plugs, changed diapers, played chess, lifted glass to lips in a score of cities on a handful of continents.

These hands will be his last view of the mortal world before his time is done.

He makes a fist, fingers trembling, flesh shaking. It does not quite close, so that the light and air still leak into the little cave made by the palm of his hand.

This lost, too, this grip. His grip on everything, really.

Once, he'd been afraid of cancer blunting him. Chemo might rob him of his mental acuity. Surgery might set him back so far he'd lose his job, his book contracts, his ability to maintain connection with friends and family. But cancer had not simply blunted the ragged man, it had blunted his entire life, edited his world into a reduced, simplified, impoverished copy of what once had been.

That word again. "Once." The true dirty word in the English language, encapsulating loss and regret and diminishment.

"Once we were happy."

"Once I was whole."

"Once I could write."

"Once, but no more."

The creative impulse had flowed like fire, in earlier days. The words found him before he could go hunting them, often as not. He'd never really understood writer's block, it had been an open road to him, until the cancer and all its outcomes had dynamited the bridges and blocked the valleys in his mind.

Writing had been like sex; like love; like a good, hard piss the morning after a night of drinking; like a baby's smile. It had been everything to him, the envelope on his life, the meat inside the sandwich, the way he made enough more money than he needed to buy the things he wanted, the path he laid down stone by stone for his daughter, for her mother, for himself.

Losing that had been almost as painful as losing his daughter. And far more painful than any of the other bits of himself he'd lost. There was no surgery scar for that, no voice-ectomy to remove his narrative sense. That loss had been softer, sadder, more quiet, more profound.

More final.

Likewise cancer had stolen his sex.

Here is a man:

```
O  [65%]     P  [1.0%]
C  [18%]     K  [0.35%]
H  [10%]     S  [0.25%]
N  [3.0%]    Na [0.15%]
C  [1.5%]    Mg [0.05%]
```

And more, of course, trace elements as there are such, impurities as it were, in any concentration of moral good or social order.

Rend a man down, boil him, strain him, dry him out, powder him, assay the result, and you will find these things. But sure as a pile of glowing coals and red-hot nails cannot be made back into a house, neither can a scattering of elements be made back into a man.

Likewise the consciousness, with its id and ego and superego and the ancient, unevolved underminds of rat and lizard and fish lurking in the dark swamps behind the eyes. Rend a mind down, strain it through terror and grief and madness and a host of ill-considered pharmaceuticals, and you will find these things. But sure as a few bubbling pots and beakers cannot be made back into a man, neither can a scattering of fragmented personalities be made back into a consciousness.

And so we can iteratively flay a person's need, ambitions, deeds and desires—organs unpacked and moved aside, passions dissected and pinned to shrivel with shame in the flickering of poorly-ballasted fluorescent lights; talents shredded down by the patient grating of pain and enforced idleness, until only the stub of a soul remains.

Everything has a weight, a value, a specific gravity. Hope, love, ambition, grief.

Everything.

Cerebrospinal fluid is the lubricant for both thought and action. The brain swims in it, the great central trunk of nerves lie within a bath of the stuff like louche canaliers in their long boats. No intention or action or recollection takes place without the stuff, and so all suffering must float down this same dark, salty channel.

1.025; URINE

[once]

Iron Springs: A tiny seaside resort on the Pacific Coast of the Olympic Peninsula. The place had outlived itself decades earlier, some long-lost interwar vision of capturing the tourist trade in the first generations of automobile travel and the American mania for roads. Moss, mold and the eternal Pacific Northwest rain had colonized the cheerful lodge and its constellation of outbuildings, a fuzzy green editorial comment on the transitory nature of man's glory in the world.

Still, Iron Springs was a destination with endless surf, trees taller than most people ever saw in their lives, dense underbrush of ferns and rhododendrons, winding paths, and quiet little cabins where secrets could be made and kept out of earshot of anyone but the principals involved.

Jay had driven up there from Portland for a writing conference. His career was going well enough for him to be invited, expenses paid, to the smaller gatherings, the places that no A-list author would bother with, but the C-list authors still paid to attend. An odd gathering of would-be writers, half-successful authors, and few fans of the process of making stories. Even the highways had gotten smaller as he went, branching and subdividing until he felt like a salmon going home to spawn. And die.

Still, it was a pretty enough day. Early summer, in the Olympics a time that felt like spring. This day was sunny, so he had the top down the whole four hours up from Portland, catching the scent of tree farms and estuaries and lumberyards as he went. He arrived to check in, and found his room waiting as planned.

No gift basket, no wine, but this wasn't that kind of conference. And he wasn't a complainer. Still, he settled easily enough into the small cabin decorated in Home Depot modern and smelling, as everything did here, faintly of mold. The view was to die for, even if the water pressure sucked. He stared through a serrated rank of Douglas firs out across the sullen, sunlight swells of the Pacific. Green forest, gray water, blue sky. Who needed the schizophrenic hues of flowers and fruits in a country such as this?

The pathways were indifferently graveled and slick with mud. He walked carefully around the grounds, breathing in the sea air. Wind plucked at his shirt, his hair, his face, questing fingers of a restless lover whose cold hands bespoke poor circulation. He could love a place like this for a few hours, or even a week. Three days was perfect.

After some time on the beach, and some time staring at the keyboard pretending to write—the words flowed of their own, Jay could no more pitchfork them from his soul than he could pitchfork his spleen from his body—he found his way to the conference's heart, in a slightly larger cabin occupied by the organizer. She was a middle-aged woman of vague memory and good intentions, who seemed to operate on the mental equivalent of duct tape and rubber bands.

"Jay Lake, ma'am," he told her. Unnecessary, surely, for she'd told him repeatedly how much she loved his books, and his face was prominent on the dust jackets of each one.

"Oh, you're *here!*" Her exclamation implied some aspect of secrecy to which Jay had not himself yet subscribed.

The door squeaked open behind him, he turned to look, and the only woman in the world walked in. She was about five foot seven, shoulder-length brunette hair, wearing a white spaghetti strap tank with the words "THIS IS SO GOING IN MY NOVEL" printed across her breasts in a declaration he was quite prepared to live up to.

"I . . ." Jay said, but even he was embarrassed at the graceless declaration of love threatening to erupt towards a woman he had now known for the longest seven seconds of his life.

"Hi," she said shyly; and he saw it in her eyes. All of it, from this moment forward— burning passion, towering stress, midnight fucks and morning tears and cooking naked in the kitchen and jointly authored bestsellers and a whole world of time and money and conferences and writer heaven in the arms of this woman.

"Yeah . . ." His words deserted him.

So the weekend went. The delicious

torture of being near her. The snickers of his students at his clumsy-as-grade-school crush. The quiet warnings dropped to Shawn about Jay's womanizing, his love-'em-and-leave-'em habits that had been legendary on the conference circuit. The smoldering almost-sex in his cabin that disintegrated into tearful talk about her husband and his affairs.

All of it unfolded into an improbability that drove Jay into his therapist's office the following Tuesday.

"I don't get it," he told Dr. Ogletree. The big leather couch was sticky under Jay's back as he sprawled across it like a Norman Rockwell painting entitled *Man Undergoing Analysis*. "Where the hell did *she* come from? Why the hell is *she* married?"

Ogletree tapped his pen on his yellow pad, cap first. With a slow smile, he launched a counterstrike—their therapy process was ever a form of warfare, YAVIS versus gray-haired cynic. "Has it ever occurred to you that the same things you find so compelling in a woman likely appeal to other men?"

"That's stupid," Jay said, then immediately regretted the words.

When he went home, he called her cell phone, the number she'd told him not to call after six in the evening.

★

[once]

The baby came early, but well enough. A delivery sufficiently uncomplicated to leave Shawn sweating but smiling through her epidural, and Jay still largely in possession of his gnawed fingernails. She was beautiful, in that manner that babies are to their parents. The nurses fussed over her, as obstetrics nurses do. Life began, as it does, nine months after a moment of sweating sweetness, and went on, as it does.

"She's so *big*," Shawn said, some weeks later. They sat on the porch of the old Queen Anne Victorian, watching the baby watch the roses watch the street outside. The yard was guarded by a perimeter of thorny-wielding knights in their bright caparisons. Color in color, from the blushing pink roses to the watery blue of a baby's eyes.

Jay nodded, playing the game. "I swear she said 'mama.'"

Shawn laughed. "Not at this age."

"She's not so big, either." He held out his hands, miming a loaf of bread. "She'd fit inside my messenger bag."

Shawn made to slap him away. "Jay!" The baby gurgled, spat, then cooed, a little machine meant to excrete poop and cute on cue, and absorb time like a black hole swallows light.

Still, she did grow. At her own pace, which is the pace of all children. And she swiftly developed a strength of character one could crack nuts on. Which, as Jay observed to Shawn on a regular basis, would make Aria a hell of a woman, but in the meantime made her a hellish child.

The strength of character masked a temper, though. When Aria was four, she threw a knife at her mother. She punched out a basement window while standing on the back of an old couch. Jay and Shawn took her into the child psych unit at Doernbecher Children's Hospital.

"You'll need to focus her anger," said the smiling young Dr. Allgood. He seemed to be fresh out of school, as if he'd just recently begun to shave for the first time. It's not that

Jay didn't trust the man, it was just that he'd have preferred a doctor closer to his own age than to his daughter's.

"What focus?" demanded Shawn, getting as she always did to the point. "She's already focused like a pistol shot."

"It's all about getting your attention," he began, but Jay interrupted—he just couldn't help himself. "She sure as hell does have our attention."

And so it went, while Aria played quietly on the floor of the exam room, a model child to all eyes except those of memory.

Still, she did grow. A constellation of storybooks and art projects and secret castles and rainbow houses lit the paths of her childhood, and it was good. The temper eased, her generosity of spirit grew, and she changed and changed again in the manner of children. All the while, Jay would occasionally see the young woman his daughter was becoming—out of the corner of his eye in the living room, passing in the grocery store. A ghost of the future, visiting to bring him a signpost.

★

Urine is the water of life, expelled with the purpose of carrying away that which life has discarded. A man undergoing chemotherapy must be careful where he pees, lest he leave behind dangerous chemicals to poison others besides himself. That rancid gold in the bottom of the toilet is a pool of regrets, undrinkable, unloved, evidence of the wearing away that erodes what is left of the patient one slow, hot drop at a time.

1.04; BRAINS

[later]

He went through a phase of making lists. Sometimes he made lists of lists, a recursive exercise that climbed the ladder of pain, as if there might be a roof to be breached, a sunlit place of calm atop the suffering and the anger and the grief. Eventually, like everything in his life, that fell away, but even much later on he would run across a scrap of paper jammed into the pages of a cookbook. A recipe for Australian shepherd's pie, with a side order of dying daughter, for example. The age of the list could often as not be divined from the degradation of his handwriting over time, the tremolos and palsies that made their home in his central nervous system, his arms muscles, his fingertips.

"No reason for it," his oncologist had said. Dr. Venturi, a no-nonsense woman just a few years older than him, who seemed to find everything humorlessly funny. He'd never thought cheerful people went into oncology.

Or if they did, they didn't stay cheerful for long. She continued, "Your brain's just fine."

That's not what Dr. Ogletree would say, he'd thought. *I may not have brain cancer, but it's definitely all in my head.*

Except of course it wasn't. Dr. Venturi was absolutely right. It was in his colon, originally. Then his left lung. Then his lymphatic system. Then, then, then . . . Another list, like the others. Sometimes it appeared on his lists of lists, like so:

- Things which are darker red than a ripe tomato
- All the pharmacies in town, ranked by distance from my house
- Supplies to fit out a child's sick room
- Years of my life without sex
- The drugs in my life, by mg dosage
- The drugs in my life, by pill count
- A boy's own atlas of needle scars
- Cancers I have known

There were other phases, too. Blogging as a desperate cry for help, spilling his guts to total strangers in the phospholuminescent privacy of the Internet, until his fans, then his friends, slowly dropped away from the endless Jeremiad of fears and complaints. He'd been a pretty good writer for a while, a minor best-seller even. But no one wanted to see inside the endless litanies of cancerbrain.

The disease really had been all in his head, even from the beginning when it was still in his daughter's body. In those years—all two of them, between her diagnosis and her death— he'd wished with all the heart he knew how to, and prayed to gods he'd never believed in, that he could bear the cancer for her.

Unfortunately, the universe had heeded his pleas. Far too late for the bargain to have any meaning. He knew he'd brought it on himself, though, through the unsympathetic magic of pain.

Shawn had remained in his life less than a year after Aria had laid herself down for the long, green-covered sleep of seasons. The love they'd found in a single moment by the Olympic coast, that had seemed brightly invulnerable, a triumph over time, experience and the errors to which all lovers are prone, had not survived the face of death. That flame had gone out like a candle snuffed in the shutting of a door.

He couldn't blame her. She'd tried so damned hard, but Aria had been hers, surely as any of his tumors had been his own. Grown inside Shawn's body, cell division and replication being nurtured by a specialized circulatory system emplaced just for that purpose. If his tumors had possessed eyes and hair, like a sideshow freak's teratoma, they would have been much the same.

Except Aria had separated without surgical intervention, drawn breath with lungs she'd made for herself, assisted by her mother, of course, and wandered into the world with her own beating heart. The children of *his* body had wound up as bloody little messes in specimen jars, whisked off through chilled white corridors to laboratories and the waiting embrace of knives and pipettes. The child of *her* body had grown in light and love to a fierce intelligent and a bonfire spirit, and an early grave.

He mourned his tumors, truly he did. But only a fraction of the depth of mourning Shawn had for Aria. Flesh of her flesh sickened and died. All he'd contributed was a momentary spurt of passion and a fraction of an ounce of sticky fluid.

Later, all the time spent, the listening and teaching and love and diapering and homework and Band-Aids—they'd shared that, of course. But only Shawn had grown Aria from a single, quivering cell.

Just as only he had grown his cancers one by one from single quivering cells. His tiny, errant children. Little homicidal mutants one and all, their bent destructive genetic programming still ultimately his.

★

The doctors had never been able to say what the cause was of Aria's neuroblastoma. Dr. Venturi had not yet appeared in his life then—Aria had been under the care of Dr. Salomon and Dr. Tung. Pediatric oncologists, a strange breed even among their curious tribe.

Dr. Salomon was a pretty woman in a very unusual way, Somali or Ethiopian or some other East African origin that Jay had never quite managed to work out and had always lacked the nerve to inquire about. She looked as if she'd been made of *thin*, stretched just slightly, so her grace was that of the crane rather than the swan. Her fingers were so long as to seem a magic trick. The light in her eyes, the humor in her voice, was only ever for Aria. When she looked at Jay and Shawn, she was always guarded.

Dr. Tung did not even pretend to cheer for the child, let alone the parents. He was an officer gone to war against the cancerous enemy. Stocky, grumpy, intense as a hot coal in a tub of vanilla ice cream, his presence oddly complemented Dr. Salomon's.

"There are less than seven hundred new neuroblastoma cases every year in the United States," Dr. Salomon said, one quiet afternoon in another of the endless parade of windowless rooms that had already come to characterize life. "Not a large enough set to justify the kind of research we'd need to really dig into this."

Dr. Tung wasn't present, off on rounds, he'd been told. Neither was Shawn. She was seeing to Aria, who had not yet managed to be so sick as to withdraw completely from the Waldorf School, though that day was clearly visible in the near future.

"Could we have done something differently?" he asked.

The look she gave him was an odd mix of pity and contempt. "Such as what? Provide an alternate genome? Or perhaps you would have proposed to raise her in a bubble?"

"No." He stared at the pen in Dr. Salomon's hand. Purple, with white letters on the barrel, advertising some unpronounceable pharmaceutical. It was easier than staring at her eyes. "I just . . . I just want to do something."

The road Aria was on now was the dead end of his soul. Jay already knew that. Losing a parent is a tragedy, especially when it happens too early, but it is the natural order of things. Losing a child, though . . .

How did people live through that, in the days before pediatrics? Just keep having babies, and hope some of them survived. He and Shawn had actually managed to speak of this, a little. They already knew there would never be another child in their lives.

"You are doing something," Dr. Salomon said quietly. "You're getting her all the help there is to be had, and you are loving her when she needs you most. In my business, we don't always win. But we can make losing as graceful as possible."

"There's nothing graceful about cancer," he muttered.

"No, truly, there is not. The grace comes from within ourselves, not the disease." She tapped up a screen on the monitor on the exam room. "I want to show you the latest bloodwork . . ."

★

Neuroblastoma offered nothing to take away. It was a systemic cancer, treated primarily with chemotherapy and radiation. Knives would bring no healing there, at least not until the metastases erupted.

His own later cancers were organ-based. Discrete tumors at least theoretically amenable to excision, whatever his own separation anxieties about his tissues might be. He became obsessed for a while with the organs themselves. Their size ranges, their abnormalities, the obvious and subtle functions of each system with the body.

Nature was clearly very conservative. An

amazing number of tasks were carried out by various tissues. Even more amazingly, people could survive without so many of them, or at least without their large portion. The systems were massively, magnificently redundant, from the genetic level up to the cellular level up to gross anatomy.

Sure, you only had one heart, but there were lungs, and a person could lose quite a bit of those and still function. The colon, in all its ropy length, could be redacted without drastic consequence. Two kidneys. The enormous maroon fist of the liver, amenable enough to being carved away and even to some degree self-restoring.

An engineering marvel, the human body, albeit a haphazard feat of effort, as if the Intelligent Designer had been blind, drunk, half asleep and divinely gifted all at the same time.

Each organ had its own properties. Weight, density, texture, specific gravity. He'd spent some time in slaughterhouses, on pretext of research, looking at pig entrails and hearts and stomachs and lungs. (He'd read on Wikipedia that pigs' organs were a reasonable approximation of their human equivalents for medical evaluation purposes.) The disassembly of a breathing, thinking—Did pigs think? Surely . . . —body into these bloody, measurable constituents was a horror and a beauty to behold.

He swore one heart had fluttered bloody and warm in his hand. Dead eyes stared with unfulfilled longing at nothing in particular. Flies, always flies, so that he was put off eating meat for months afterward.

But the organs, disassembled, spread out, arranged in a map of the interior. If only the rage, the terror and the grief could be so cut away, sliced apart, separated, analyzed, weighed, measured. What was the density of fear? What was the specific gravity of grief?

Rubbery veins caught between his fingers like overcooked pasta yielded no particular answers, but then, he had not expected them to.

★

Another list, this one entitled "The Things I Shall Lose." Some of the items have been ticked, or crossed off, as if being accounted for by an auditor of pain.

~~Control of my bowels~~
✓Use of my cock
~~Control of my finances~~
~~My job~~
✓My heart
✓My marriage
~~My writing career~~
~~Friends~~
✓The future
~~Hope~~
~~Love~~
Understanding
My life

★

Jay's greatest success had been with a novel series about a crippled werewolf. Noni the Crooked, who was the lycanthropic equivalent of a little person or a Jack Russell terrier, born with achondroplasia, then later wounded when the Carmine Council destroyed the wizard bar-Simon in an epic battle outside Paducah, Kentucky. Noni walked with a limp, and perpetually spoke to women's breasts because that's where his eye level was, but his heart was solid and his burning sense of manifest injustice, combined with the still formidable powers of even a crippled werewolf, had earned a fan appeal so strong that it had shocked Jay, his agent and his editor.

Ginny Harrison had called him up after the second round of royalty statements came in. "Jay, I just wanted you to know, these numbers aren't a mistake."

He had the papers in his hand. 147,224 net copies in trade cloth, which was to say, hardcover. "On a good year I move 30,000 hardbacks," he said. "We live off mass market paperbacks." Jay honestly had not paid attention to the print run on *Limping Under Silver*, the first Noni book.

"Not this time." She sounded almost joyful. "We're amending the contract for book two, and they're committing to books three and four."

"I was planning to write another Elventree book." He felt stupid as soon as the words left his mouth. Noni was outperforming his established fantasy series by a factor of five hundred percent.

"Write all the Elventree books you want, just write Noni first. I'll keep you off the hurry up program. That will give you time to explore. Just don't do something to ditch your numbers."

Meaning, *quit writing little crap and act like the bestseller you are now.*

Jay valued Ginny because she told him the straight story, without ever getting on his case. She didn't need to. The woman had a way of being exquisitely polite even when she was handing you six yards of rope and directions to the gallows.

The weirdest thing was, Noni had literally begun as a joke. Something said in a bar one night at a convention, writers trying to top each other with stupid ideas. "He's a one-armed veterinarian with uncontrollable Tourette's syndrome, she's the first girl Pope with a rubber-latex fetish; together they fight crime!" That sort of thing. A crippled little person werewolf had fit right into the beer-fueled laughter of the evening.

Then that night he'd actually dreamed of the poor little bastard. Noni was getting the shit kicked out of him by a gang of high school kids, and trying to crab away. Finally the physical stress had bumped him into the Change out of time, a fight-or-flight reflex taken to a new edge, and he'd still been short and funny looking, but now he was short and funny looking with four-inch claws and a set of fangs that would have made a shark think twice.

Thing was, Noni didn't go for the Bruce Willis moment and tear the kids limb from limb. Not in the dream. He'd smacked them around some, just to slow them down, then he'd cocked a leg and pissed on all five bullies, before bounding over a fence and high-tailing it into the mists of a golden afternoon.

The dream sequence had been too schmaltzy and downright inane to be used in fiction straightaway, but a version of it had been the hook on which he hung *Limping Into Silver*, and it had survived into the final production manuscript.

A joke and a silly dream, and now he was looking at, what, a hundred grand in royalties?

How the hell could that be possible?

Ginny was talking, saying something, excited. Translation rights, movie rights, a big audio book offer. Jay just said yes to everything, to let her work it out, then went and found Shawn to tell her the great news.

A week later, Aria came down with the fever that would lead to neuroblastoma and settle her into the earth within two years.

After a while, Jay never wrote again. After a while longer, he never published again.

There is a thing that happens inside the mind of a writer. It is similar to the channel that visual artists open, or musicians, or black belts, or anyone who works in the zone, past the edges of conscious competence and deep into the uncharted countries of inspiration. Similar but different.

Story lies at the heart of everything it means to be human. Our deepest ancestors feared the fading of the moon and the winter passage of the sun, and told themselves why the light would return. Narrative—*mythos*—undergirds every aspect of the human experience from birth and the first suckle at the breast, to the last dusty gasp by the yawning grave. God spoke the world into being, Odin sacrificed his eye for words of wisdom. That lightning rod from the casual-but-serious act of speech down into the racial memory, the species overmind, changes the storyteller as surely as any surgery might revise the body of a man.

Everything acquires meaning. The world is newly made of bright brittle edges and fuzzy clouds of context. Odd turns of phrase, a rose left to rot in a doorway, a pretty stranger's smile on the street—any of these can trigger a cascade that unfolds into plot, story; fraught with meaning or perhaps just laced with simple laughter.

So when things go wrong for a writer, their internal observer continues to chronicle, take notes. A writer dying of a heart attack will dictate to his closest friend the sensations, the pain, the aching arch inside their chest, until the EMTs or death come to take away the words. A writer trapped in a well will note the daily passage of the sun and the smell of her own breath decaying, waiting to recount it if she is ever rescued. A writer with a sick child will analyze, externalize, chronicle and displace with the tools at his command.

Until something breaks.

Until cancer, the ultimate (anti)social disease, reaches out with its rotting claws and snaggle-toothed jaws to rip apart the fabric of that writer's life, steal the precious treasures of his heart, and leave him grieving, broke, lonely, and worst of all, mute.

★

How to write a story

A List, by Jay Lake

1. A character in a setting with a problem

A man lies bleeding with a hole where his heart used to be, his body eaten by disease.

2. The three-act structure is hard wired into human consciousness

A rabbi, a priest and an oncologist walk into a bar.

3. Remember the details, all of the senses, even kinesthesia

Nothing ever smells like a hospital, not even your grandmother's bed sheets.

4. Watch your language. Word echoes echo wrong

"Brutal words for brutal times," said the bullet-headed god with eyes like rivets and all the conscience of a drill press.

5. Be honest rather than consistent

my pen is a knife, my heart the joint upon the plate before me

6. Bleed on the page

Too late to do otherwise

7. Dialog dialog dialog

"No one wants to hear this shit. It's depressing, and we all cope with death through the pretense of invulnerability."

"Bull crap. You're a maudlin, self-indulgent twat who'd rather moan about his life than get up off the floor and deal."

"You want these fucking tumors? Take your choice! Cancer of the spirit, or multiple metastases eating your body from the inside. Every time I get up off the

floor to deal, some fucking surgeon cuts off another piece of me!!!"

"If you keep talking like that, no one will love you."

"There's not enough left of me to love. Strip away the limerence and the fascination, and all that's left is scars to pity."

8. Learn through failure (the character as well as the writer)

We are the sum of our failures. Success is nothing but the error rate in the failure stream. Entropy is the rapist reaper of us all.

9. Payoff

Same payoff as ever there was. Shovel bites dirt, someone weeps, a bird flies past uncaring. The sun never paused in its course for anyone's broken heart. Why start now?

★

[eventually]

Cancer is the story of what it means to be human. We are born to die, the disease is just an unusually detailed itinerary of the journey between those two moments of cold surprise.

Imagine this scene:

A man walks into his doctor's office. She's an older woman, bit of a stick, hides behind her statistics and her stethoscopes. Still, like most doctors, she is there for the patients. No one goes into transportation medicine for the laughs.

"Doc, I've been hearing these strange growlingnoises. Mostly at night, right when I'm falling asleep."

"I assume you don't have a dog," she asks. It is her little joke, and the patient understands this as such.

"No, ma'am, no dog. Just growling."

"Let me pull up your charts, Mr. Lake." She taps at her keyboard a little while, the screen angled just far enough away from the man that he can't quite see what she's doing. "Hmm. Interesting."

You do not want to be *interesting* to your transportation medic.

"Fluid levels are consistent with protemporal omnibus syndrome. And that cross checks with your tread wear patterns."

"I'm sorry, Dr. Valdosta, I'm not a clinician, I don't understand."

She taps her purple pen against the keyboard tray.

"Let me put this another way. You have a seventy percent chance of being fatally hit by a bus in the next year. The growling noises are its engine as it heads towards you. The event is reaching back to you across

time. This is typical for some classes of transportation

fatality, I'm afraid."

The man is horrified. "My god, what can I do? I'm, I'm not ready…"

"Well, we can hardly stop all the buses," she says reasonably. "Think of the impact on the economy. I *could* put you in crosswalk therapy. That will improve

your odds, especially if you're diligent about jaywalking."

"I can't really help that," he mutters, but already he can see the end coming. The map of his future has been opened before him, and it is shorter and more sad than he ever imagined, even in his darkest moments.

Everyone pretends they cannot see the appointed hour and manner of their death.

And it is a truism, borne out in concentration camps and grade school classrooms around the world, that people can get used to anything. But that ever-speeding decline, that hurtling towards irrelevance which we normally allow to old people confined to malodorous beds and pretend among ourselves will never happen to us; well, when it does happen to us, we young, healthy, vital people who will never grow old and never die (so the lie says), what then?

The sum of all fears, and an erroneous division by zero.

Cancer is the story of what it means to be human, because it is the chart of death as surely as birth and childhood are the chart of life. Yes, some people cheat the reaper. Doctors are clever, and their medicines are sly. But cancer is clever too, a demon traveling on a bloodborne highway and thinking its secret thoughts in the silent crevices of the body. It has a way of coming back, again and again, until one year you don't get lucky on the scan, and the fleshy flowers bloom too brightly to stamp out this one last time.

And in truth, is that any different from the way of all deaths?

- Hit by a bus
- Choked on a fishbone
- Hemorrhagic fever
- Drowned over the rail of a
    storm-tossed tuna boat
- Jailhouse riot
- Gangrene
- Stage III Alzheimer's
- Embolism
- Jealous lover
- Simply giving up

Sometimes, though, you go on fighting, regardless of the odds.

★

The true home of cancer is in the mind, and the true home of the mind is in the brain. Brains, so soft and salty, stirred with a spoon, churned by a tumor, salted with grief until they are useless for all other pursuits, even love. Poisoned before chemo ever hits the veins, scarred before the scalpel ever touches flesh, it is the brain that suffers first and cries out at the last.

1.05; SOFT ORGANS

The ragged man shuffles on. Cold bites at him differently than it used to. There is far, far less of him, for one.

The mother of his child had loved him for his size. So she'd said, back in those early years. He'd never quite understood that, and he does not understand it now, how such a lithe, beautiful woman who could have literally her pick of lovers and life partners, found such fascination in his oversized, sloppy body.

He is still sloppy these days. All the more so, in truth. But oversized? No, not so much. The ragged man looks down at the memory of his belly. The skin still hangs flabby, a sort of desiccated fleshly apron which he sometimes catches sight of in the bathroom mirror. But the rounded smoothness he carried for so many years is carved away, starved away, melted by drugs and time and a permanent loss of appetite.

She would not approve, if she were still present in his life. One problem that had solved itself.

Losing the fat, the mass, the shape of him, had opened him to the biting wind, and invited in the chill. Even worse, his first course of chemotherapy had upended his temperature sense in a way that never seemed to have repaired itself. Cold was now torture, instead of annoyance. FOLFOX-Avastin was unkind, though not as unkind as some chemo regimens.

Still, the ragged man can not stand to avoid the outdoors. Rooms do not hold him any more. His spirit is whittled to a nub no larger than a matchstick, a long, slow reduction from the towering redwood he'd once secretly imagined himself to be. Likewise his body, slimmed past even the manic false logic of bulimia into a skeletal echo of himself. Reduced, diminished, he needs all the space the world can give him. It is as if his soul fits nowhere smaller than beneath the dome of the sky.

"Cancer has made me large," he whispers to a pair of beady-eyed crows. "But I do not want what I have got." Suspicious corvid regard turns briefly to an alien, avian sympathy before they fly away in a burst of feathery sound.

The sidewalk consumes him as well. Never in life was he forced to pay such close attention to the falling of his feet. The ragged man is medically fragile now. A stumble can mean time in the hospital. More things are fatal to him than he can account for.

So he does not account for them. He simply has a care, and refuses to stop moving forward. Death of his child, devastation of his heart, four rounds of surgery and three of chemotherapy, and still he moves forward. He does not know what else to do. Backward is impossible. We are all time travelers, advancing at a steady pace of one second/second, and no one has yet found the key to walking the other way.

Even if he could, what of it? The ragged man used to write science fiction for the magazines, though his trade novels were exclusively fantasy. He could construct a scenario where he goes back in time and does . . . what . . . precisely?

Avoid meeting the mother of his child at Iron Springs? The resort would be poorer by a few room-nights, and his life would be poorer by glorious years with her.

Avoid fathering and birthing his daughter? He cannot imagine never having held her at all, even if his last hug was in her coffin. It is not as if he could somehow control her genetic tweaks to make the neuroblastoma afflict some other family in some other time and place.

Live in a different house, a different neighborhood, a different city? Were the cancers environmental? Almost certainly not, inasmuch as the mechanisms of cancer are ever correctly understood. But a high fiber, vegan life in the unpolluted countryside might have spared them all *something*.

His putative time machine would do little except enable him to relive both glory and grief. Nothing would change. The ragged man has long since determined that he prefers his memories. To do it all again . . . He could not stand that.

So instead he shuffles on, attentive to cracks in the sidewalk and small sticks and mossy patches that might slicken the sole of an unwary shoe. Balance is a tricky negotiation these days, simply because of the prices his body has paid and continues to pay.

He wonders sometimes why the God he does not believe in has chosen to spare him thus far. Early on, in his second cancer, a Christian friend had said all unbelieving, "I don't know how you do this without faith."

The ragged man had no answer then, and he has no answer now. What would faith boot him? Someone to blame? A God so malicious and uncaring as to allow his life to be eaten away? Or solace, perhaps. But what solace in a saving force so indifferent to suffering. He is the Problem of Evil, on two feet. Not so much in the Hiterlian sense, but more in the Jobian sense.

A just and loving God would either have spared the ragged man his family and his dreams, or crushed them all at once. The extenuated, attenuated limbo that his existence has become is punishment beyond even the worst sinful, excesses of his youth.

Long ago, when he was fat, happy and colorful, the ragged man used to joke that perhaps it was his purpose in life to serve as an example to others. While he still believes that might be true, these days he is more inclined to think that his purpose in life is to absorb the pain of others. A modern day sin-eater, with cancer the bread of error.

Around him, his friends and family went from shock to pity to grief to fear, until they fell away one by one. He could not blame them. Too much tragedy becomes farce, and no one wants to be center stage when the whitewash bucket drops for the fifth or sixth time. Without the child to bind them close, and exhausted by his own endless travails, they had all drifted away.

So, as he began life, the ragged man finds himself alone, here at the overdrawn, long extended end of his life. Bereft of adipose tissue, riddled with scars and holes and chemical damage, limping through the streets of his adoptive city with the sound of hooves echoing in his ears as the pale horse always follows close, close, close behind.

[always]

Fear is the ultimate teacher. Sometimes it teaches us swiftly, a sudden final lesson punctuated by death. Sometimes it teaches us softly, a whispering voice gnawing at the tendons of the soul as night passes into day and day returns to night. Sometimes it is simply a hard taskmaster, as when cancer is the rod of correction in the dread hand of fear.

There is so much to fear in cancer. The obvious. Death. Pain. Suffering. The inane, soap opera drama of a life at risk, steely-eyed doctors with their gazes glinting over face masks in a desperate race against time and hope to save the deserving patient.

The truly insidious aspect of cancer is the creeping agony that breeds fear like a kitchen sink breeds bacteria. Because cancer, usually, is *slow*.

Prostate cancer can be so slow that it takes a lifetime to kill. At the other end of the spectrum, pancreatic cancer can kill swiftly enough to seem like a blow from the fist of God. But most cancers take time.

Time to be conceived by cosmic ray or environmental toxins or the miserable accidents of genetic chance.

Time to birth in the subtle errors of cell division and the small failures of immune response.

Time to grow like small children playing

inside the vesicles and vacuolae of an indifferent, doomed giant.

Time to be noticed by a vigilant scan tech.

Time to be considered, discussed, analyzed, planned, plotted against.

Time to go under the knife while chilly operating theatre air startles you and some machine hisses you into a small, dreamless precursor of the death that is to come.

Time to awaken in the long twilight agony of surgical healing and mind-blunting opiates.

Time to be told what the pathologists with their little jars and microscopes found.

Time to have a port installed in your body, so that you become a mild hybrid version of a cyborg, a Terminator sworn only to avenge yourself by slaying your tiny, errant cellular children.

Time to lie still while vile drugs that would constitute poisonous assault and insult to the body by any other means drip into your veins to rob you of what remains of your vitality.

Time to wonder and wait in sick dread.

Time.

Time.

Time is the razored edge on cancer's sword, the throat-slitter, the nut-cutter, the breast-riever, the eye-gouger, the wrist-slasher. And in the end, time takes us all, whatever dread demon might wield it.

Slow, slow time is the greatest weapon in cancer's arsenal of fear. It is the general guiding strategy in that civil war within your body, on behalf of the dark forces multiplying their cellular hordes.

The lesson cancer teaches with that instrument of time is this:

You never have more than today.

We are all time travelers, and we all abide in the eternal now. There is no past, only memory. There is no future, only anticipation. The moment that exists is *now*. Always, always now. Cancer poisons memory and voids anticipation and fills the now with pain and violence and grief and anger and a hundred other manifestations of fear, but mostly what it does is fill the now with waiting.

Now is the most precious commodity any of us have. We trade it away, second by second, cashing it in for recollection and the endless duties of the day, and occasionally, power or passion.

So you learn from fear the true value of now. You learn that you never have more than today.

★

[once]

When Aria was dying, Jay mostly held it together. Not Shawn, she'd let her grief run free from the beginning. They'd fought about that. A lot.

"You're mourning her, and *she's not gone*," he'd hiss, late nights under the covers in their big old bed that had once been his grandmother's. Children had been born under the watchful oversight of that oaken scrollwork, and old people had died. Now the bed simply hosted sleeping, and fucking—though much less of that lately—and more often now, fighting.

Stress will out.

"I am *not* mourning her." Shawn rolled over, presenting him the curve of her back. It was the ultimate abandonment (at least back then) that he could not simply gaze into the dark amber depths of her eyes as the two of them talked their way through whatever was bothersome.

They'd talked their way through everything from the very beginning. Sometimes disagreeing, rarely arguing, never fighting. Just using their words. Never fighting until now, until the unthinkable had stolen the heart out of their love.

"She knows," he said. He couldn't help himself, the words would not stay decently behind his teeth. "She can see it in your face."

Shawn's next words floated muffled by clutched sheets and the uncrossable distance of her body. "And you've handled it so well, haven't you? The perfect father!"

Jay hated that scorn. He knew it wasn't really meant for him, that his ears were standing in for the indifferent deafness of Aria's neuroblastoma, but he still hated that scorn, was still hurt by it.

"I'm keeping calm for her." He pitched his voice quieter, as close to soothing as he could come in that moment of this conversation. "Confident."

"You barely look at her."

She was right, as she always was. Every time he did look at Aria, he saw the woman she should have become, and now probably never would. So he looked at her memory instead, as often as possible, focusing his eyes on his daughter's hand, her shoulder, the spoon by her untouched bowl of vegetable broth. "I love her," he said simply. Stupidly.

At that, Shawn began to cry, and would not be comforted by his awkward hands or tentative words.

★

[once]

The real fear—the Fear—came later, during his first round of cancer. Colon cancer, which had presented unexpectedly with a series of violent, bloody bowel movements the day that *Limping Under Silver* had been released in mass market paperback. *Splinter From the Elventree* had done well enough in mass market, and the Noni book had been a genuine bestseller in hardback, so that his agent and his publisher had already gone from hinting around to explicitly suggesting that maybe writing another book would be both therapeutic, and lucrative.

The first eruption had occurred when he'd woken, around 5 am, so he'd scuttled into early clinic hours at the hospital. They'd poked him a bit, done some bloodwork, and sent him on his way with the admonishment to return to the Emergency Department if the bleeding continued.

But the day was busy. Jay had not yet understood he was done with writing. Or more to the point, that writing was done with him. He'd driven all over Portland that day, to the various Powell's Books locations at Burnside, Hawthorne, Cedar Hills. Even the airport Powell's, outside of security where anyone who wanted the joys of mall shopping and the airport experience in one convenient package could go without needing to clear TSA. He'd also hit a lot of the Barnes & Noble outlets in the area.

It was always fun, talking to booksellers and section managers and the occasional random reader.

He'd spent a lot of time in bathrooms, wondering what was wrong and putting off the hassle of going back over to the hospital and presenting himself at the ER. It wasn't until that night, sprawled on his couch poking fingers into ghostly conversations via Instant Messenger that he'd mentioned all of it to one of his friends, who'd practically come unglued in chat that he hadn't gone to the ER hours and hours earlier.

So he'd gone, and gotten a hard lesson in triage techniques—never arrive by car if you actually want to be seen, and try to arrange your blood to be visible, because secret blood left by the pint in toilets every twenty minutes isn't as urgent as someone with a cut lip that the admitting nurses can see.

The lesson had been nearly fatal. When he'd finally been admitted, some five hours after arrival, he collapsed just inside the doors with blood pressure too low to measure. That Jay hadn't been straining out another bowl of blood when he'd passed out to die on the bathroom floor was a not-so-minor miracle.

So the medical establishment had done what medical establishments do. They swiftly determined, from comparing his morning hematocrit numbers to a rush job in the emergency room's lab, that he'd lost twenty-five percent of his blood volume that day. Theories were bandied as he was stabilized, admitted to the hospital, treated for causes unknown.

The hospital brought flashbacks of Aria in quiet rooms with pulsing machines and eye-wearying light. Shawn was gone by then, and he hadn't been up to calling his friends and family. Jay had spent enough of the past two years being an object of pity. He didn't want more of it now. So he'd suffered quietly until the gaggle of doctors came on many feet to speak in many voices to tell him of the cancer in his colon.

And then he'd finally understood Shawn's fear. The fear he'd bottled up inside himself all through Aria's illness. The great, bone-shaking shudder rising up from deep within, that stole breath and pumped tears and knotted his gut. The knowledge that things would never be the same—*again*—that his life was being stolen, the crime already committed, and he was living out the sentence as if he were both victim and thief.

Small consolation that the cancer would eventually die with him. It was a mute beast, devoid of hopes and dreams and ambitions and a laughing smiling daughter and a beautiful loving wife.

All of which had been subtracted from him as well, leaving him with only fear, and Fear.

Later, through the many laters that infested Jay's life after that day, he would find himself driving, in his vanity keeping the top down, and having to stop at the side of the road and sob. Or stand up from some task, walk to the couch, and curl upon it in an orgy of near-terminal regret. The Fear stalked him like a cat on a cockroach, cancer's proxy that had taken up residence in his soul, and resisted all attempts to be evicted.

Sometimes it disguised itself as grief, or rage, but the Fear always came back to tears and terror. The only other emotion remaining that was genuinely his was self-pity, and even in his worst moments, Jay would not allow that. He'd written this on the back of an old drawing of Aria's, a decently-wrought dragon flying over a forest:

Fear teaches, grief releases, rage inspires.
Even they have their good sides.
Self-pity is just another form of poison.

His daughter might have been an artist when she grew up, her sense of composition and eye for form was so strong, even in the lower grades. She'd never reached the upper grades, died in the year that would have been fifth grade if she'd lived on healthy.

Jay knew he should have died, but the other gift of the Fear, by strange paradox, was to prolong his life within its questing coils.

"Things I miss," he wrote:

- A woman's skin like raked velvet beneath my fingertips
- A good hamburger
- A bad hamburger
- Catching my breath
- Walking in the mountains
- Sleeping without pain
- Bacon and eggs

- Sex
- ~~My words~~
- ~~My wife~~
- ~~My daughter~~
-
-

That list was on a torn off piece of a kraft paper grocery bag, the kind the stores only gave you grudgingly now. The other side read simply, "ON'S", and he'd scribbled there over time perhaps a hundred little tiny cartoon eyes. Sometimes he considered adding to the list, had even gone so far as to leave lines in place to receive his future regrets, but the losses of the present almost always seemed to be sufficient without requiring him to amend them with even more misfortune.

The softest organ is the heart, and never mind the specific gravity of muscle mass, nor its density. The heart can collapse under its own weight, like a body from which the bones have been stripped, until all that remains is a fleshly engine pumping blood inside the hollow body of a man.

1.0621; BLOOD

"Flesh of my flesh," Jay said. He stood at the graveside in the rain. The cemetery was stupidly beautiful, which was so very wrong. They ought to be blasted, withered places, to match the scarring so fresh upon the souls gathered there. "Blood of my blood."

Shawn stood nearby, but not too close to him. She hadn't quite left, not yet, but they both knew it was all over. Neuroblastoma had severed the bonds of their love as surely as it had severed the bonds of Aria's life.

"She was our daughter."

He'd meant to use simple words, to make his case before an indifferent God and an uncaring universe as plainly as possible. But they sounded maudlin now to his own ears. The mourners around him rustled and coughed, a many-legged beast trapped in the Oregon rain until he released it. Like a spell, the eulogy.

"She was our pride."

Would he have this many at his own funeral? He doubted that. Aria had been un-usually popular, for a ten-year-old.

"She was the world, and the world should have been hers."

Shawn stirred at that, but he wasn't sure why. Jay was trying very very hard not to look at the too-short coffin, just as his wife had accused him of not looking at Aria when she was still alive, but barely.

"We gave her life, but we could not help her keep it."

The words got away from him now, his prepared remarks disintegrating in a slow tsunami of grief which threatened to roll him away in the rain's cold embrace.

"We failed her, as parents. We failed to protect her long enough until she could learn to protect herself."

He hadn't *meant* to say that, and the crowd did not like it. His father's eyes, the gaze of a man who'd once been able to stop, and perhaps start, wars around the world, flashed hard. The meaning was clear enough: *What the hell are you doing? Don't screw this up, too.*

"Today we bury our only child, my parents' only grandchild, and we bid farewell to a generation of hopes and dreams."

Sorry, Dad, I don't know what else to say. The words have carried me away.

"I would like to tell you to dream on, to continue hoping, to tell you that Aria would have wanted it so."

All eyes on him, some sad, some shocked, a few, worst of all, pitying.

"But I would be lying. I am done with hopes and dreams."

He tossed a book into the open grave, Noni's adventures inscribed to his daughter, then walked away from all of them while behind him, someone else stammered through the necessary final words to release the spell.

★

Cancer weaves a bubble around the patient. It is a tiny cell, nearly solitary confinement, though exposed to all the world. Lonely but never alone. Piteous but never pitied. Lovely terror without terrible love.

The bubble is visible but transparent. Some patients wear the pink hat, the yellow wristband, carry their cancer with pride into the world. They use words like "remission" and "survivor." Others are quieter, more subtle, the bubble visible only in a pain line on a young face, or the echo of fear in a haunted glance.

But there is also a strange fellowship among those who live inside these bubbles. This one with her cervical cancer has shared fear with that one with his intestinal cancer. Not so much shared stories, though in the manner of people at all times everywhere stories are swapped, but shared experience.

Surgery is bad enough. People who have gone under the knife for any of a million reasons can understand the unreasoning terror of anesthesia, the spirit-sapping seduction of opiates, the slow hours and days in a hospital bed while machines measure out your life in milliliters that drip drip drip by with all the deliberation of an executioner checking the straps on the gurney.

But the fear, the grief, the rage ... those are the province of cancer and its bubble, shared down to the bone and soul only by others in their same bubbles.

Surely this is true of AIDS, or diabetes, or

multiple sclerosis. Surely every sufferer carries their own bubble. Cancer is not special. Cancer is almost normal, a gift of evolution and the body. "Surprise," the genes say. "You didn't want life to be this simple and easy, did you?"

Lucky we are whom biology loves enough to gift with this special purpose, to be the fascination of oncologists and the source of regretful warning to friends and relatives and even random strangers on the street. "See," the cancer whispers, "this can happen to you. No matter how virtuous or vile. No matter how clean you live or foul your sins. No matter your weight, or the endless hours of running, your diet of pizza or oat bran, the color of your eyes and the rating of your sunscreen. This can happen to you. Look upon my works, ye healthy, and despair."

Still, the patient in their bubble finds friends with common purpose. In the hospital ward, in the infusion center, at the support group meetings, out in the text-laced thickets of the Internet. Cancer is a secret bond between strangers, like a Masonic ring, one that confers immediate mutuality and a strange, honest species of trust.

We all die alone, but the same bubble that cancer uses to isolate and kill us also introduces us to a strange, twilight society of transients.

So perhaps, you might reluctantly conclude, another of cancer's lessons is this:

We are not alone.

Such a strange, hard teacher to produce such an ordinary insight.

Jay wrote a poem during his first round of chemotherapy, when the side effects of the FOLFOX-Avastin cocktail were keeping him indoors far more often than not.

> I miss the cold air upon my face
> I miss your hands upon my body
> I miss walking free for hours
> I miss her sleepy irritation in the morning
> I miss jumping up from my chair
> I miss your embrace
> I miss my innocence
> But I repeat myself
> Still, I miss my innocence

That poem was a prayer to the cancer god, that heedless deity who took away almost everything and gave so little back. No one sane would pursue wisdom by this path, but sometimes wisdom was thrust upon its sufferers. The cancer god, a divine magpie, thieving away every bright and gleaming thing from a life, leaving dull pebbles behind.

He'd thought to open the doors of grief on the wings of story. To fly away from the prison of his heart using the words which had been so long his to command. Spinning fantasies wasn't just second nature to Jay Lake, it was what he *did*. But even when he sat at the keyboard, so little came. Not constipation so much as the empty gut of starvation.

The beast that lies at the heart of every writer had been slain by cancer, and he had done nothing to raise it from the dead. The disease came back to claim his attentions again and again, first on Aria's body, then on his own flesh, until he could no longer pay attention to anyone or anything but the fearful pain of it.

The thing Jay resented most about cancer was the *narrowing*. It made him small, over-focused, took him away from everyone and everything in his life. A friend had once referred to him as a "typhoon of varied interests." Cancer became its own interest, as all-consuming as booze to an alcoholic, and no less destructive.

"I was great once," he wrote on another scrap of paper. This one he later burned in his shame, but still he wrote. "I could command a thousand people from a microphone, or ten thousand from the printed page. Now I cannot even command myself." He'd drawn a little picture of a tumor, small and blotchy and livid with evil.

Still, the cancer god stalked him, toying with him. It took away everything, but not quite his life. Then it let him come creeping back a while, before it took away everything again. But still not quite his life, though at times he prayed to the stinking, alien god to claim that too.

Only the illusion of choice remained, in the wake of the disease. Only the pretense of volition, free will, of anything but obeisance to knives and drugs and buying another few months or years of life by trading away everything he had and everything he held dear.

He tried, once, talking to it directly. This was when Jay could still drive, before he'd sold his foolish red convertible to an eager high school boy with dreams of big scores in the back seat. He'd driven out into the Columbia Gorge. Already too weak to make a long hike, the car carried him well enough up to Cloud Cap, the upper head of the Tilly Jane trail on Mt. Hood, where he'd been able to stumble far enough at altitude to find privacy on a wind-swept basalt boulder.

There he laid out the tools of his prayer—the slice of colon his surprised doctor had reluctantly given him after the initial operation, preserved like a withered segment of banana in formaldehyde. Beside that, the pathology report from his first tumor. A certified copy of Aria's death certificate. A photograph of him and Shawn at Iron Springs, taken by someone else's camera but already capturing what they had so firmly believed to be deathless love. A twenty dollar bill and an airline bottle of scotch, because no self-respecting god could go without such offerings.

Jay laid these out on a rock and studied them a while. The words long-considered and long-rehearsed would not come. Finally he resorted to the beginnings of that unfortunate eulogy.

"Flesh of my flesh," he told the wind. "Blood of my blood." Was the damned god even listening, or did it only heed the zipping and unzipping of genes? The words began to flow. "I have failed everyone, most of all myself. Please, take it back. Please, return my life to me. I have already paid too high a price. There is nothing more."

The wind had no wisdom. The rocks brought only cold. Eventually he drove home, weighed down by one more defeat.

★

Blood carries oxygen and nutrients around the body, an express delivery service whose cargo is life itself. But blood is also the highway for eager metastases, cells roaming toward a new home and a crippling fate. Savior blood, traitor blood, no wonder those Christians worship you so in your sanguinary glory.

1.085; MUSCLE

[now]

The ragged man shuffles back into his little apartment. Two rooms, a bed, a brutal toilet not cleaned as often as it might, because bending over is difficult. He keeps the place warm, though that means he does not have quite so much money for food. Little enough is left to him, but he clings to life, and to be cold is to be dead.

So many of the indignities visited upon cancer patients by their doctors come amid cold. The chilled air of operating rooms. The brisk bite of needles. The temperature sensitivity conferred by chemotherapy.

His muscles are as ragged as he is. Never an impressive specimen, he at least once had bulk, girth, mass, presence. The ragged man no longer remembers why this part was allowed to waste away, why that piece vanished on its own. His scars he can number surely as a Galileo could count the stars in the sky. But his body?

So long since vanished from being his own.

Even now, this deep into the fading story that is his life, the ragged man still makes lists. Sometimes they are trivial:

- `Milk`
- `Oatmeal`
- `A banana`
- `Salt`

Sometimes they seem profound to him:

- `Aria`
- `Shawn`
- `Dad`
- `Myself`
- `Life`

Mostly they are just placeholders.

Dr. Venturi has been emailing him again. His days of keeping a stable of technology in his home are long behind him, lost in the economic collapse and permanent destitution that is the lot of anyone in America stricken with indefinite illness who was not already independently wealthy before their downfall. As a result, he must go to the library or a coffee house to read these most private, written conversations.

He does not keep all his appointments these days. That is the ragged man's slowest surrender, the abrogation of diligence that is for a man with his medical history surely as much a suicide as any bullet taken by mouth.

Theories have abounded over the years. Radiation poisoning, though impossible to tell where from, and besides, his cancers did not particularly conform to the bone and thyroid disorders expected from such pathology. Environmental contamination was always his own pet theory, that would explain Aria's death and his own, in the context of a family history blessedly free of cancer but notably marked by cardiovascular disasters in each generation. Unusual gene complexes, autoimmune disorders, something like allergies, viruses, cosmic rays, alien encounters.

Did it ever matter? Not from the beginning.

Dr. Venturi has become as much a confidante as a physician. These days she writes him long, rambling notes about advances in treatments, and how they map to his own history. Liver cancer suspected three separate times, but disappearing again from the scans, as if the tumors had blossomed and remitted all on their own without medical intervention. The elusive state of his lymphatic system. The confirmed cancers in colon (surgery), lung (metastatic, surgery, a single chemo course), lung again (primary that time, surgery, two separate chemo courses), and prostate (radiation, followed by surgery).

He is a minor medical mystery, a walking case study. His treatments have subsided to scans, and maintenance drugs. No one really wants to slice him open again, or pump him full of violent reactants and heavy metals yet another time. They bring medical students into his exams, his charts carefully studied, to touch his scars as if he were a pagan idol and learn something. The ragged man is never sure what.

He has survived, so far.

He does not particularly expect to survive much longer, though he has been wrong in this matter before.

He finds he does not mind so much either way.

So he misses an appointment or two. Skips a scan. Doesn't bother to file the appropriate paperwork with the hospital, with the state. Sometimes he forgets he has SSI money in his tiny bank account.

Instead he walks. Slowly and not far at a time. But he walks, and emails Dr. Venturi about the flight of birds and the way the wind worries at the maples in the park. Sometimes he remembers to mention his pain levels. He stopped talking about his fears years ago.

Dr. Ogletree is gone from his life too, these days. Therapy seemed so pointless, and when the ragged man's insurance coverage collapsed down to the essentials of public assistance, too far out of reach.

But there is a girl at the coffee house who smiles at him when he orders his tiny hot chocolate—the one indulgence in the ragged man's life, both the drink and the smile, when he guesses her shift right. He even knows her name, as she has a Mickey Mouse hat with "Susquehannah" embroidered on it propped above the cash register when she is working.

The ragged man holds her name a secret, pretending his hasn't seen in written before his eyes, or perhaps hoping it is not the sly joke of a too-young, too-hip girl named Kayla or Mei Ling.

But she does smile, as if she's glad to see him. And she remembers his name, which was slightly famous once, though she has no reason to know that. Susquehannah is a bit older than his daughter would be, had she lived, and so he also likes to pretend the two of them might have been friends.

He always tips her a quarter, which she is wise enough to recognize for the mean extravagance it is, and is gracious enough to thank him for regardless. In time, he wanders away, but he has yet to catch her looking after him.

That is just as well.

★

Fear is a living thing. A cancer of the mind, coiled around the heart. Some people swallow whole and keep it choked down behind clenched teeth until they die of rot.

Others let it run free in an endless chatter, until they become sick of their own words, their own terrors, their own needs.

The social disease that is cancer is a vector for fear. It infects parents, lovers, friends, neighbors, the clerk at the post office, the cashier at the grocery store. Fear moves from mind to mind, heart to heart, relentless as any killer flu virus. Nature is not so much red of tooth and claw as black of fear and terror. The epidemiology of fear would make a study to fill libraries.

Yet even fear serves a purpose. Even fear motivates the weak, gives pause to the head-strong, and forces the sturdiest mind to review its purposes. It lives, parasitic and dangerous, but still bearing a germ of worth within its dark-fanged grip.

★

He said a lot of things, when Aria fell ill. He said a lot more things when his own cancers first began. Just as a man might cry out in desperation as the first shots echo over a battlefield, so Jay did.

Much later, when he was ragged and obscure and prematurely old, abandoned and forgotten by friends and family, Jay finally recognized that he had driven them off far more than they had left of their own accord. Love refused eventually does fade, no matter what the stories might say. Some of them written by him, in fact.

Cancer had stolen his reason from him as much as anything. It was trivial to state that all men were mortal, born to die, living between that first sharp scream and that last sigh. It was quite something else to feel it.

He'd been so lacquered by the grief of Aria's illness, and her subsequent death, that Shawn had nothing left to grip on to. Lacking a handle, she'd drifted away, as she used to say when she rode astride him, shouting that he must hold or down or she'd float into the air.

Shawn: A woman-balloon, glorious in her gorgeous nudity, set free to float writhing and moaning above the streets of Portland, her passion drizzling down in a gentle, sensual, pheromonal rain.

He wondered where she'd gone, what she'd done. Shawn was a writer too, in truth a better one than he, though he'd begun his career earlier, and so they'd met in part as mentor and student. If he still had a computer at home, any interest in the Internet, he surely could have found her by the trail of her work.

But at the coffee house he was always too charmed by Susquehannah, or too blued by her absence, to think of such things. And at the library, well, that was depressing for other reasons. The Multnomah County system still carried some of his books. He didn't like to think about that.

So now he was alone, Shawn drifted away, Dad frustrated and even older now—when was the last time he'd spoken to the old man? Not having a telephone was both liberating and limiting. The friends who had tired of chasing his depressions and his angers and his griefs and his fears had found more rewarding pursuits.

"It was not the cancer did this to me," Jay told the tiny, dusty, too-warm apartment. The walls had no answer, though his little lists pinned and taped everywhere carried hints. What could he do now? Too late to start over, too much lost to pick up where he'd left off, but he was bored with pain, bored with waiting to die.

He opened the Maxwell House coffee can where the extra money lived. "Extra" for a fairly limited value of that word. Forty-seven dollars and seventy-five cents, it was. Money rolled in his pocket, he bundled up to go outside, taking the bus pass he mostly used to go to the hospital and back and headed for Goodwill.

It was time to find a typewriter and revisit the words that had fled him some years ago. Back to the beginning, when his first keyboard had no screen at all, just clattering keys and impacted paper, wounded by the dark ribbon ink and the thrusting of his fingertips.

Muscles articulate the bones, and enact the intention of mind and spirit. The meat of a man, they are as vulnerable to genetic error as any other part of the body, but some seem more left out. Muscles carry a man to and from a shoddy store. Muscles slowly and painfully tote a secondhand typewriter into a small apartment. Muscles put paper onto the roll, strike the keys, type a few words centered in the top half of the page, followed by a familiar name.

Muscles lead the rebellion against a generation of loss.

1.5; LIVER

The ragged man's liver is the greatest battle-ground that never was in the chronicles of his cancer. The disease has played ghost-in-the-attic with him and his doctors time and time again. He considers this ironic, given his own general indifference to drinking the attendant classic ills of that organ.

The ancient Greeks believed that the liver was the seat of thought, and emotion. He is not certain they were wrong. His temper over time has been by turns bilious, sanguine, phlegmatic, even tortured. All of those states seem to have arisen from his relationships within.

Sometimes he imagines glistening brown arches towering over rushing rivers of blood, a sponge designed by H.R. Giger, a fluid filter for all the poisons in his body. Chemo hit the liver hard, stressed it as it tried to keep up with the flow of drugs and chemical violence. He might as well have been a drinker, with the heartbreak of cirrhosis to show for his efforts.

Yet sometimes he also wonders if the liver, properly motivated and coached, might not have been able to filter the cancers from his body. The immune system rises out of the bone marrow, in a piece of marvelous cross-engineering that is the delight of biologists and doctors everywhere. But surely the liver, in its appointed tasks, can recognize the invaders for what they are, daughter cells of the body turned coat and taken up arms against their host.

The ragged man even went through a period where he sketched livers on napkins and the backs of junk mail envelopes, and one self-pitying night, on his own raddled skin with a black magic marker.

Still, the cancers played seek-and-go-hide through that large, difficult organ, and even while marching through the ragged man's system, seem content to leave well enough alone.

The cancer god has always been there. He is a god of vertebrates, of evolution, of any creature lucky enough to have a complex metabolism shared among constituent cells. He is endlessly patient, for his day will never end until all days end. Unlike most gods, he is not sustained by belief. Rather, the cancer god is embedded in the very fabric of reality, his name written in the letters and words that pick out the genomes of every species that walks his world.

He knows he will always win, in the end. Some may die of disease or predation or starvation or competition or cross-town bus, but always he will receive more offerings. They give themselves up to him, his creatures, and he takes without mercy, for mercy is not the purpose of cancer.

Neither is grief, if one truly lives in the now as animals do. Grief is a specialized form of recollection, specific in its gravity, and one must possess emotional memory and the ability to long for that-which-was. The cancer god does not feed on grief, and those are not his prayers.

He feeds on ringing of the suffering changes, the disintegration of order, the prorogation of error. The cancer god is entropy incarnate, a death prayer written in our genes. Even immortals who have cheated death fear him. Certainly everything that ever walked or swam or flew this earth would quail at his name, had they only ears to hear it and mother wit to recognize him for who he truly is.

He is *us*, life, Mother Nature's alter ego, and the price of evolution. Without malleable cells, we would never have come into being. The cancer god is father to us all.

Surgery hurts like fuck. There is no other word for it. Anaesthesia holds its own special terrors, transcending reason, but the invasive opening of the human body is a profound violation of the natural order of things, a shock that is felt for months and years after. Only the fact of an even more profound violation is enough to move the surgeon to her knife, and still the patient is prone to weep with fear.

Surgical prep is always chilly, conducted in cold rooms by quiet-eyed anaesthesiologists. The epidural is strange and frightening, a stab into the spinal nerves that seems like such a betrayal of self. The screening questions, the light banter, the long slow roll through the hallways toward an operating theatre—so much time to fear, to come unglued, to babble and sob and beg to be permitted to wake up again when it is all over.

The only real blessing is the retrograde amnesia that masks the final minutes before surgery, so that your memory is of an empty room filled with equipment, not of masked faces and gloved hands and the closing around like crows on a corpse.

But after. Oh, after. The sea of pain. The life raft of opiates. The little indignities of catheter and glucose and saline and PICC line. All the tiny, pointed agonies, the body refusing to unbend, the mind refusing to engage, the long, dark hours barely breathing as the monitors bleep out the little threads that keep you alive.

Surgery is so terribly lonely and cold and painful. Like death, except if you're lucky you get to go home again.

★

[eventually]

He moves more slowly just lately. Something is winding down inside him, though he is barely into his fifties. Surgery, chemo, pain and fear have subtracted from the tally of his years. The ragged man has long since given up worrying overmuch about death. Even pain has become a familiar, bitter friend. As for time, whatever bargains he made in ages past have been shredded on the altar of the present.

The ragged man truly does live in the now. Like a cat, or a seed perhaps. His potentials are spent, pissed away in a river of drugs and blood and urine, but he remains.

With his little bundle of typed papers— for the typewriter itself is too heavy to shift easily, and he wonders how he managed to bring it home in the first place—the ragged man sets out for the coffee house several days a week now to edit his work under the bemused eye of Susquehannah. It is an excuse, finally, to linger among people longer than the drinking of his hot chocolate or his forays into his Gmail account.

He times his visits for her shifts, as best as

he understands them. If the Mickey Mouse cap is not on the register, often as not he turns away and struggles back home. Spring has become summer, so walking is not so difficult as it has been for months. Summer is the season of his heart, as well, and for the first time in years, something blooms.

Not the girl, for she literally can be his daughter, and almost his granddaughter, had he been inappropriately precocious. But she reminds him that there were women in the world. Women always were his taste, and a smile, a welcoming arm, a time at the breast had been among his great comforts when he was younger and less raddled and had something to trade for that they actually wanted.

And in truth, there had been two women in the world, for many years. Shawn and everyone else. Now as Susquehannah smiles at him, her short dark hair flicked back her face, he seems to remember Shawn more.

Why had he let that go?

His daughter. Aria. Life had splintered in the face of her illness, then fragmented in the face of his own. He had pushed them all away, as much to spare them as anything.

Shawn. Dad. His writer friends and his old school friends and his hang around at the bar friends. Pity was never enough force to climb the wall that he'd built around himself.

How could one compass the death of a child and the death of self in the same lifetime? And from cancer, that ancient, implacable enemy.

He'd taken all the lessons from grief, but none of the healing. He'd taken all of the terror and all of the fear, but never really passed through that next door.

"I was wrong," he tells Susquehannah one day over his hot chocolate and his twenty-five cent tip.

"Not you!" she says with a laugh, and smiles so sweetly her dimples make his heart ache.

"Never let go of the people who don't want to let go of you," he tells her. Then, in a fit of honesty, adds, "That's your random bit of advice from a weird old guy for today."

"You're not weird," she says, serious now. "And you know what?"

His heart skips a bit, somewhere between hope and terror. "What?"

She leans over the counter. The ragged man is a gentleman and will not will not will not look down below her chin where her grubby oxford shirt falls open in what ten or fifteen years ago would have been an invitation. So focused is the ragged man on not looking that he almost misses her conspiratorial whisper.

". . . who you are."

"Who I am?"

"Yes." She grins now. "I found you in the library. If I buy one of your books, will you sign it?"

Smiling, nodding, making excuses and agreements, Jay stumbles away from the counter to sit at one of the three Internet terminals this coffee house boasts. He has not signed a book in six or seven years. He has not written one in eight.

"No," he mutters with a look at the sheaf of typescript still in his hand. "I tell a lie."

Time is not his friend, but time has never been his friend, not in the years since Aria first fell ill. There was always less and less to do, a narrowing, until he has lost everything but what lay within. He knows this as surely as he knows the maps of the IV scars upon his body, as surely as he can name his tumors and their sites.

Weeping a little, but too tired to do more, he sits at the terminal and Googles up Shawn's name, looking for her for the first time in years.

He has a Gmail account. He can write her a note. It will not hurt. They never really said good-bye. And if he is very lucky, she might be willing to say hello.

On his way out the door, Susquehannah calls, "See you later, Mr. Lake."

He turns, gives her the last ghost of his old smile from the good days, and slowly makes his way home with a sense of hope, for the first time in years.

Another list, because lists are important. This one is entitled "Things man cannot live without."

- Love
- Stories
- Air

- Water
- Food
- Each other
- Himself
- Shawn

★

The liver is the only organ that can regenerate itself. Consider what that says about its importance to the human body, which can grow neither brain nor heart beyond what is given at birth. Heavy, too, nearly as dense as bone, it weighs down your chest and mine. Dark and patient, scrubbing our sins, it is the most loyal soldier in the ragged man's fractious, mutinous metabolic army.

2.01; BONE

At the last there is only bone. All lessons learned, all hearts broken, church bells fallen silent in the healing rain. Does it matter if this one was claimed and that one was spared? Bone survives, a while at least, as char in the crematorium, as the underpinnings of the corpse on the student's table, as the last to melt coffin-bound beneath the gentle ministrations of sweet mother entropy and her microscopic servants. Sometimes bone survives clad in flesh, walking the world another season or score of years.

The specific gravity of grief cannot be measured. But cancer can be heard, learned from, taken inside and transformed in the crucible of a wounded soul from a travail to a gift. Not a gift you would offer to your worst enemy, if you had one.

Neither love nor medicine can defeat death. Still, love endures, medicine progresses, and grief, well, grief is the price we pay for being born into the world. At the grave, no paths are easy.

Somewhere, the cancer god smiles, and turns away from tear-stained prayers. Somewhere, a child is born, cold and surprised. Somewhere, two people fall in love. Somewhere, a tumor begins. Somewhere, a scalpel cuts skin. Somewhere, damp bones molder quietly amid the bright and tiny dreams of insects.

Somewhere, we are all human, and none of us are alone.

That is the lesson of cancer.

ABOUT THE AUTHOR

Jay Lake made his SF/F publishing debut in 2001. A prolific writer, he had more than 300 stories published and ten novels published, with others in the works. He won the John W. Campbell Award for Best New Writer in 2004. He was a multiple nominee for the Hugo and World Fantasy Awards, and was also nominated for the Nebula, Sturgeon and Sidewise Awards.

In 2008, Jay was diagnosed with colon cancer. Jay never backed down in his quest to demystify cancer and blogged extensively about it.

Jay lost his fight with cancer on June 1, 2014. His final collection, *Last Plane to Heaven*, came out shortly after his death. It won the Endeavor Award in the fall of 2015.